Bambi

One spring morning, there was great excitement in the forest.

Animals and birds hurried to welcome the new Prince. His name was Bambi. He was the son of a noble stag, the Great Prince of the Forest.

Bambi lay fast asleep by his mother's side.

When he woke and blinked his eyes, the little spotted fawn saw happy, smiling faces all around him.

"My name's Thumper," said a friendly rabbit. Bambi smiled.

It wasn't too long before Bambi was ready to explore the forest.

Mother Quail and her nine babies passed by. "Good morning, young Prince," they called.

"Good morning!" cried another voice above Bambi's head. He looked up and saw a mother opossum and her three babies. They were hanging by their tails from a tree branch.

"The forest is a wonderful place!" said Bambi to himself.

One day,
Bambi and
Thumper were
playing happily
together. Birds
sang and fluttered
over their heads.
Thumper pointed
at one and said,
"That's a bird."

Bambi
repeated the word,
"Bird!"

Then a butterfly fluttered by. Bambi
called out, **"Bird!"**

"No," giggled Thumper, "that's
a butterfly."

Bambi turned to a pretty flower and
shouted, **"Butterfly!"**

Thumper laughed. "No," he cried, "that's
a flower!"

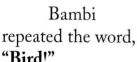

Bambi bent down to smell the flowers. Suddenly, a small black and white head popped up from under the petals.

"Flower!" said Bambi, again.

"That's not a flower, that's a skunk!" Thumper laughed.

"That's all right," the little skunk said, shyly. "He can call me Flower if he wants to." And with that the three new friends left to explore the forest together.

The days passed happily for Bambi. One morning his mother took him to a new place – the meadow.

The meadow was wide and open and covered with flowers. Bambi's mother warned him that they had to be very careful. "There are no trees here to hide us," she said.

Bambi ran off into the tall grass to play. Soon, he found a little pond. He leaned over and looked into the water at his

own reflection. Suddenly, another reflection appeared. It belonged to a female fawn about the same age as Bambi.

The female fawn smiled at Bambi and wagged her tail in friendship.

Bambi felt very shy. He ran back to his mother and tried to hide.

"It's all right," Bambi's mother said.

"That's Faline. She just wants to be friends with you. Go and say hello."

Bambi went back to Faline. They chased each other around the meadow. Soon, the two fawns were laughing and playing hide-and-seek in the tall grass.

Just then, a group of stags charged across the meadow, led by the Great Prince. He had come to warn the deer that there was danger nearby.

As the deer dashed towards the trees, Bambi couldn't find his mother. He began to panic. The next moment his father was beside him.

Bambi followed the Great Prince into the forest and was overjoyed to see his mother was there too.

Later that day, Bambi asked his mother what the danger had been. "Man was in the forest," she told him.

Summer and autumn passed and the weather grew colder.

One morning, Bambi woke up to find the world had turned white! Bambi's mother saw his surprise. "That's snow," she said. "Winter has come."

As Bambi walked out into the deep, crisp blanket of snow, his hooves sank into it.

The young fawn was having great fun making hoofprints, when he heard Thumper calling him.

"The water's stiff!" called Thumper. "Come on, you can slide too!"

Bambi rushed over to join him. But his hooves were too small to balance on the slippery surface. He fell onto his tummy with a loud – **THUD!**

Thumper showed Bambi how to balance on the ice. Soon, the young Prince was gliding gracefully across the pond too!

Winter was fun at first, but as time passed by, there was less and less food. All the animals grew hungry.

Eventually, there was nothing for Bambi and his mother to eat except the bark on the trees.

One day, when the air felt a little warmer, Bambi and his mother went to the meadow in search of food. There they found a small patch of green grass peeping out of the snow.

Bambi and his mother ate the grass hungrily. Suddenly, Bambi's mother looked up and sniffed the air. She sensed danger.

"Go back into the forest!" she ordered 'Bambi. "Quickly! Run!"

Bambi raced across the meadow with his mother close behind him. There was a loud – BANG! "Faster, Bambi, and don't look back!" his mother shouted. As he ran, there was another loud – BANG! Bambi was too terrified to look back. He carried on to the forest, where it was safe.

Home at last, Bambi turned to look for
his mother. But she was not there.

Bambi's heart thumped with panic. He
called out again and again, "Mother! Mother!"
The little fawn began to cry.

Just then, his father appeared by his
side. "Your mother cannot be with you any
longer," he told Bambi, gently. The Great
Prince would now protect his son until he
could look after himself.

As the months passed, Bambi grew into a fine young stag.

One sunny spring day, he, Flower and Thumper were strolling through the forest together. Suddenly, Flower spotted a pretty female skunk. He crept over to her and the two animals giggled as their noses touched.

"Oh, no! said Thumper. "Flower's twitterpated! Owl said it happens to everyone in the springtime!"

"It won't happen to me!" Bambi said, firmly.

"Me neither," Thumper agreed.

Minutes later, a lovely female rabbit hopped over to Thumper. He was delighted.

"Twitterpated!" sighed Bambi, as he carried on alone through the trees.

Bambi stopped to drink at a small pond. A soft voice said, "Hello, Bambi." He turned round and saw a beautiful

female deer. It was Faline, his childhood friend.

Faline leaned over and gently licked Bambi's face. He was surprised at how much he liked it! He'd become twitterpated too!

Just then, a young stag called Ronno appeared and shouted, "Faline is coming with me!"

Bambi knew he had to protect Faline. Lowering his head, he charged at Ronno.

A fight began! Again and again the two stags charged at each other.

Although Ronno was stronger, Bambi was determined to win. With a mighty toss of his head, Bambi finally threw Ronno to the ground.

Ronno limped away. Now, Bambi and Faline were free to begin their new life together.

The warm days of spring and summer passed happily for Bambi and Faline.

Early one autumn morning, Bambi was woken by a strange smell.

He climbed to the top of a cliff, high above the forest. He could see smoke in the distance. Just then, his father came up beside him. "Man has returned," he said. "Those are his campfires. We must go deep into the forest – quickly!"

Bambi rushed back to warn Faline.

He found her trapped on a cliff ledge. A pack of angry hunting dogs snapped at her heels.

Bambi rushed at the snarling dogs, Faline managed to escape and ran towards the river.

Bambi fought off the dogs and turned to follow Faline. Suddenly, he heard a loud – BANG! He felt a terrible pain in his shoulder and fell to the ground.

Bambi was too weak to move, and suddenly he saw flames coming towards him. Man's campfires had set the forest on fire!

"Get up, Bambi!" a voice cried. "We must go to the lake. Follow me!" Bambi opened his eyes and saw his father beside him.

The young Prince struggled to his feet and followed his father through the burning forest.

Eventually, the stags came to a huge waterfall and jumped. Down and down they fell, crashing into the water far below.

Bambi and his father waded through the water and headed towards an island. Many other birds and animals had already found shelter there.

Faline was there too. She was overjoyed to see Bambi again and gently licked his wounded shoulder.

Safe on the island, the forest creatures watched helplessly as the fire destroyed their homes.

When the fire finally burned out, the animals returned to the forest.

After a long, hard winter, spring arrived. New grass and flowers grew where the fire had been. The forest was beautiful once again.

One warm morning, all the animals and birds came to see Faline and her two new fawns.

Standing nearby was their proud father, Bambi, the new Great Prince of the Forest.